RUSSELL AYTO PRESENTS...

Cats are skilled catchers of mice and other pests.
Robbers are not. They just rob. – R.A.

BLOOMSBURY CHILDREN'S BOOKS
Bloomsbury Publishing Plc
50 Bedford Square, London, WC1B 3DP, UK
BLOOMSBURY, BLOOMSBURY CHILDREN'S BOOKS and the Diana logo are trademarks of Bloomsbury Publishing Plc
First published in Great Britain 2019 by Bloomsbury Publishing Plc

Text and illustration copyright © Russell Ayto 2019

Russell Ayto has asserted his rights under the Copyright, Designs and Patents Act, 1988, to be identified as the Author/Illustrator of this work

A catalogue record for this book is available from the British Library

ISBN: HB: 978 1 4088 7651 0; PB: 978 1 4088 7650 3; eBook: 978 1 4088 7652 7

1 2 3 4 5 6 7 8 9 10

Printed and bound in China by Leo Paper Products, Heshan, Guangdong

All papers used by Bloomsbury Publishing Plc are natural, recyclable products from wood grown in well managed forests.
The manufacturing processes conform to the environmental regulations of the country of origin.

To find out more about our authors and books visit www.bloomsbury.com and sign up for our newsletters

RUSSELL AYTO

CATS AND ROBBERS

BLOOMSBURY
CHILDREN'S BOOKS
LONDON OXFORD NEW YORK NEW DELHI SYDNEY

Inside the house, everything
was as it should be.

Outside, everything
was not.

The house was being watched.
Spied on by **three** robbers.

"One big old empty house . . ."
said Robber **One**.

"Equals lots of loot for us!"
said Robber **Two**.

"Hmm, let's see,"
said Robber **Three**.

They **spied** through
the windows . . .

and **spied** through
the letterbox.

Then the robbers checked
their **robbing list.**

Paintings?

"RUBBISH"

Sculptures?

"USELESS"

Vases?

"CRACKED"

Sweets?

"STICKY"

Safe?

"Splendiferous"

"Superior"

"FULL OF LOOT!"

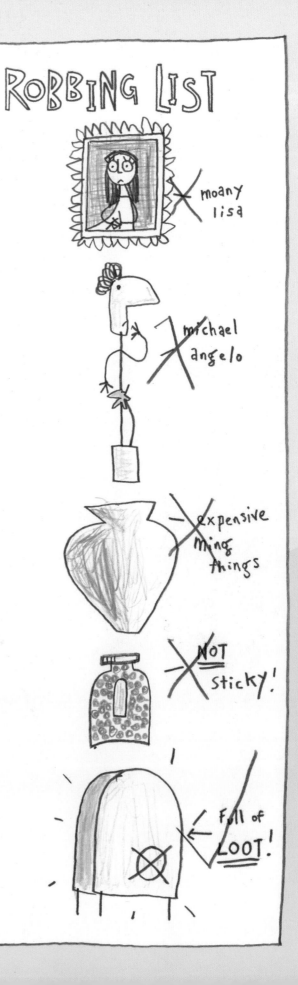

But,

from

somewhere

deep

down

inside

the

house,

the

robbers

were

being

watched . . .

Spied on by **two** cats.

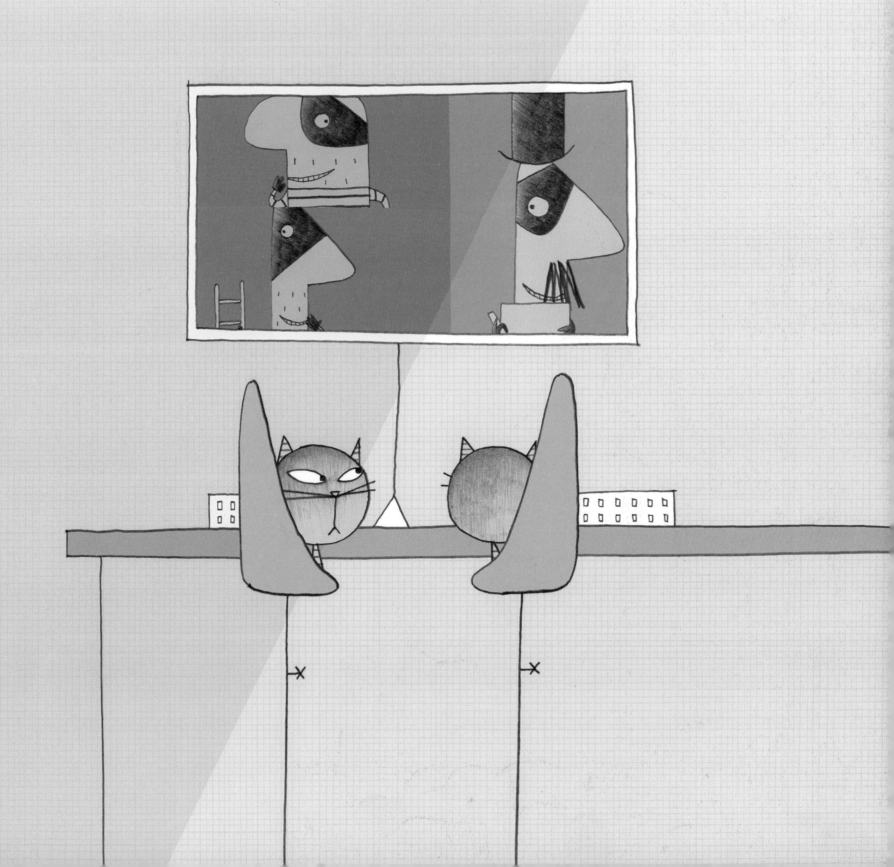

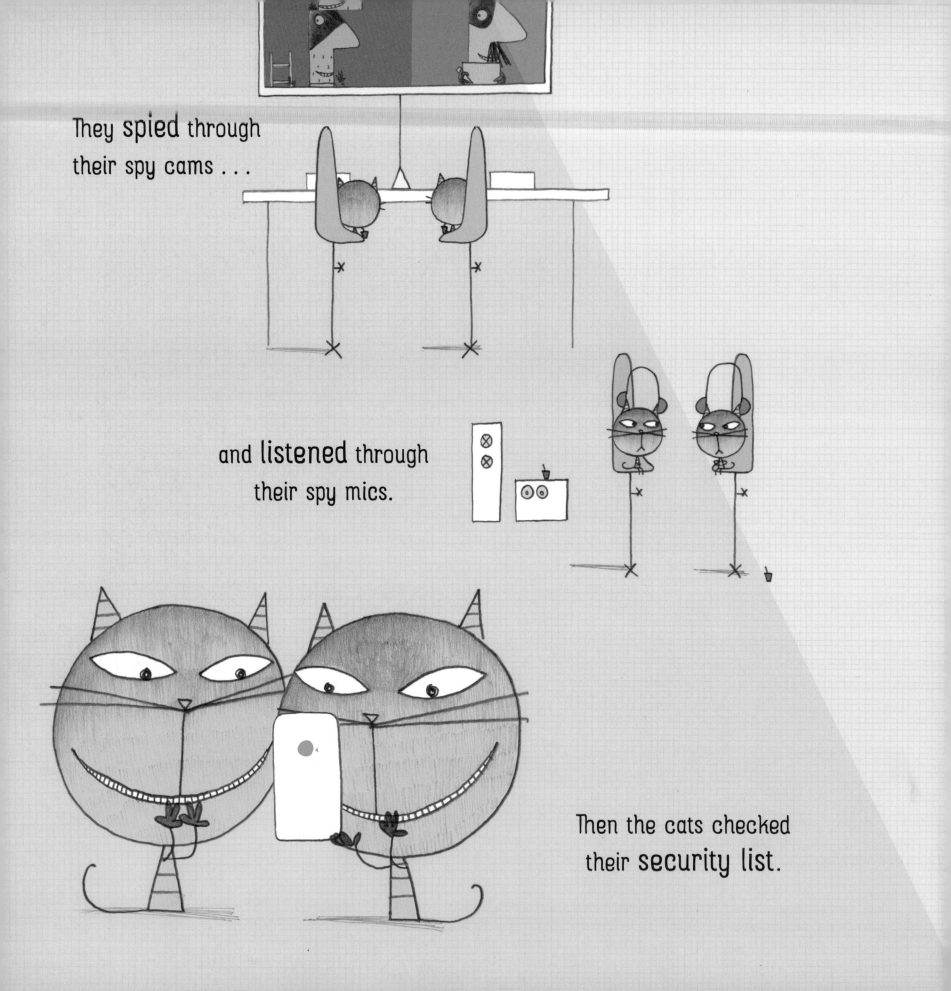

Springs?

"SPRINGY"

Litter tray?

"FULL"

Cat flap?

"SET"

Carrier crate?

"SECURE"

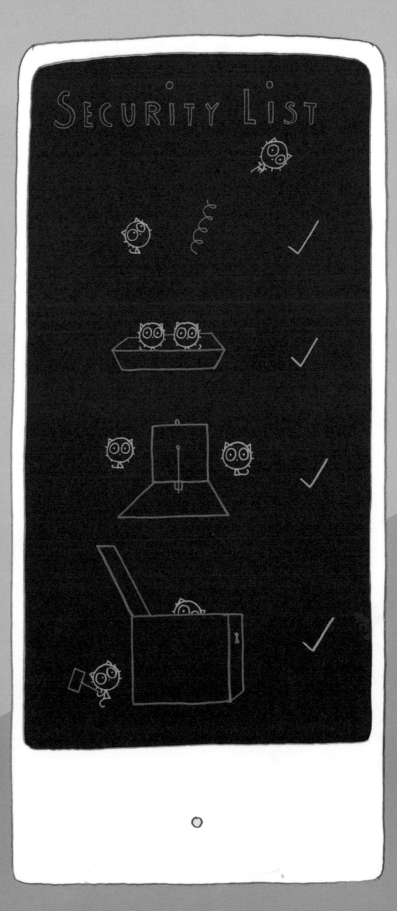

Sometime later, not quite
the middle of the night,
the robbers started tip-toeing,

tip-toe,

tip-toe,

tip-toe.

Until . . .

went the **spring-loaded paw claw.**

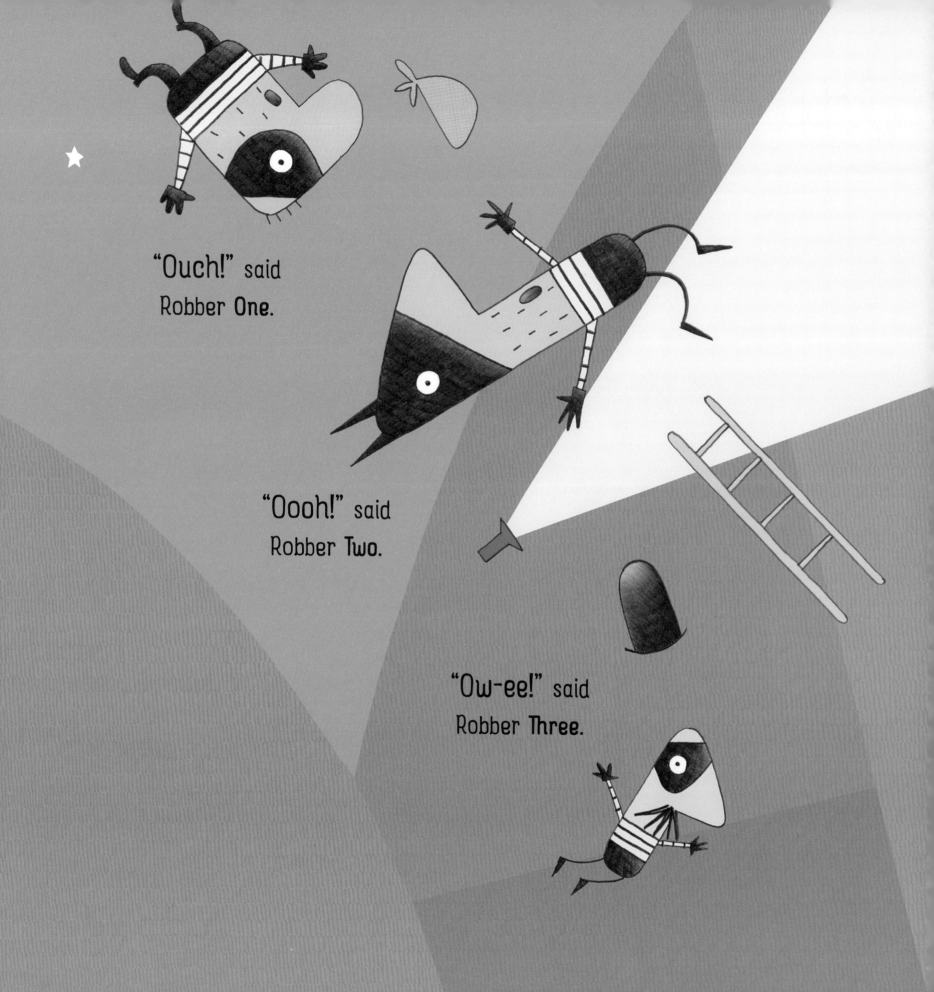

"Ouch!" said
Robber **One**.

"Oooh!" said
Robber **Two**.

"Ow-ee!" said
Robber **Three**.

The robbers started sneaking,

sneak,

sneak,

sneak.

Until . . .

PYONNNG!

SPLAAT!

went the litter tray launcher.

Next the robbers started creeping,

creep,

creep,

creep.

Until they were peeking,

peek,

peek,

peek,

directly at . . .

the SAFE!

"It's splendiferous!" said Robber **One**.

"It's superior!" said Robber **Two**.

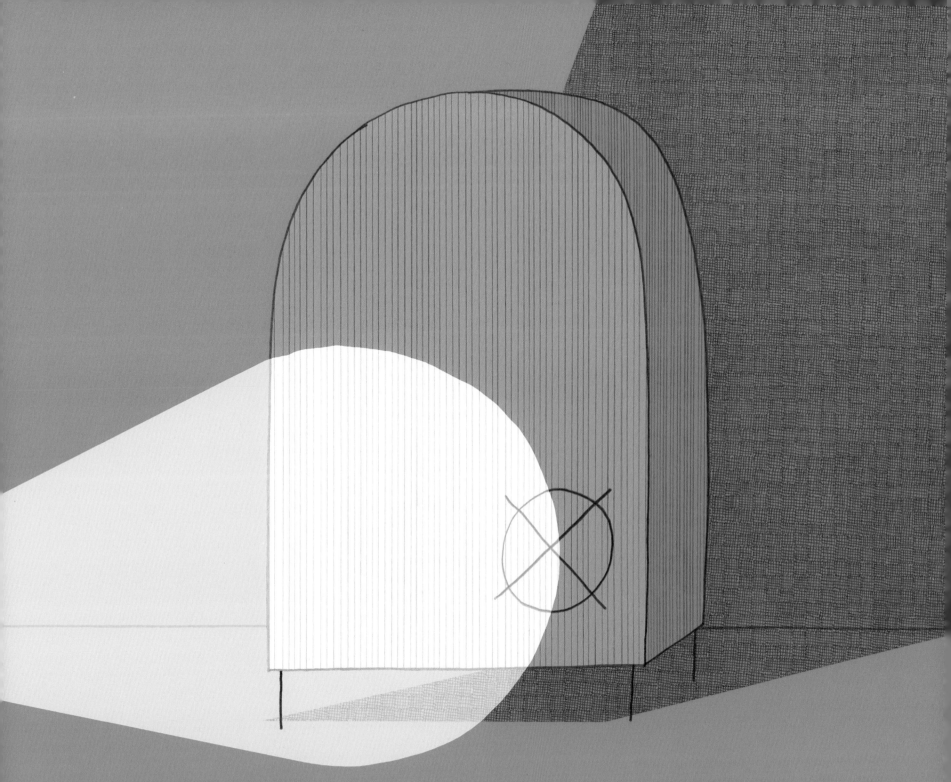

"And it's FULL OF LOOT!" said Robber **Three**.

"NOW BLOW THE DOOR OFF!"

But . . .

**WHIRR!
CLICK!**
went the

cat flap

booby trap.

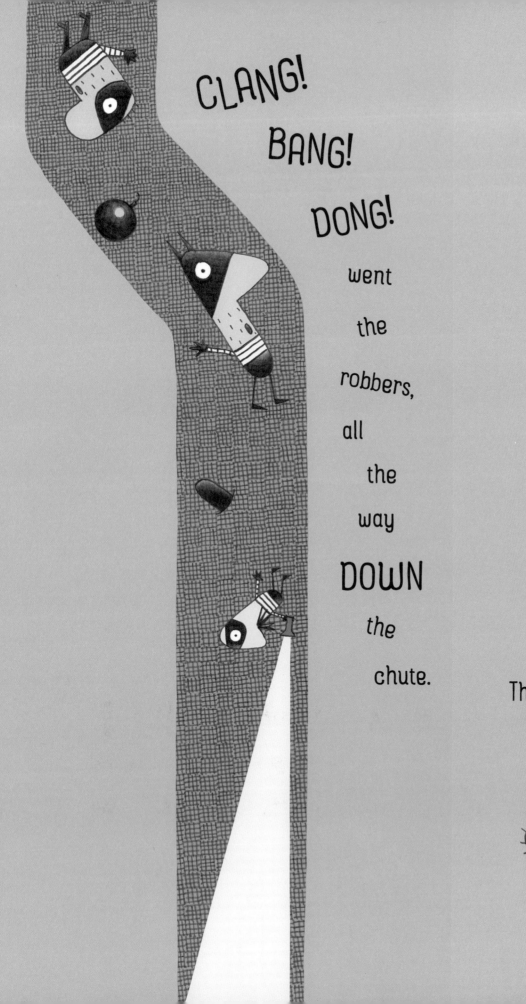

CLANG!

BANG!

DONG!

went

the

robbers,

all

the

way

DOWN

the

chute.

Then . . .

SLAM! CLUNK!

FOR THE POLICE

went the **escape-proof carrier crate.**

"Drat!" said Robber **One**.

"Rats!" said Robber **Two**.

"NO," said Robber **Three**. "CATS!"

Sometime later, not quite the middle
of the day, the little old lady came back.

Outside the house,
everything seemed
as it should be . . .

Inside, everything was not *quite* right.

"Hello pusskins. I hope you haven't been
up all night **catching** things again,
have you my dears?

Now, what about your **breakfast** . . .

"Hmm, let's see."